Great Depression Era, 1929-1941

In 1932, Tennessee-born Hattie Wyatt Caraway (1878-1950) became the first woman elected to the U.S. Senate. She represented the State of Arkansas until 1944.

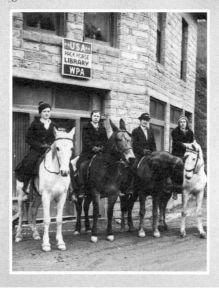

This WPA project in Kentucky was known as the 'Pack Horse Library'. Unemployed librarians were hired to travel into remote parts of the state by horse and mule. They brought saddlebags filled with books to grateful readers.

An unlikely racehorse named Seabiscuit—seen here winning a race in Baltimore, Maryland, on November 1, 1938—won the hearts and imaginations of fans across America.

On December 7, 1941—a 'day that will live in infamy'—Japanese suicide pilots raided Pearl Harbor, Hawaii. Their surprise attack on the United States Pacific Fleet brought America into World War II.

1936　1937　1938　1939　1940　1941

Severe dust storms like this one on April 15, 1935 in Boise City, Oklahoma, intensified Americans' economic difficulties.

In the 1936 Olympics in Berlin, Germany, Jesse Owens (1913-1980) won the most gold medals at the Games—four—angering Germany's Adolf Hitler.

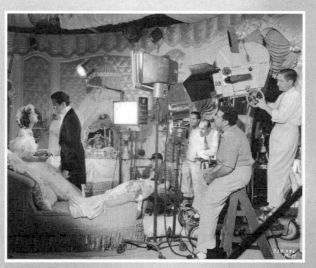

Movie set of the 1936 movie, *Camille*, starring Greta Garbo (1905-1990) and Robert Taylor (1911-1969). Movies provided escape and inexpensive entertainment during the 1930s.

This relief sculpture on the Louisiana State Capitol in Baton Rouge was one of many public works of art created around the country by artists employed by the Works Progress Administration (WPA) during the 1930s.

For John Whitman, in appreciation—Jo Harper and Josephine Harper

To Emma and Anne: You will always be found!—Ron Mazellan

Turtle
BOOKS

Finding Daddy: A Story of the Great Depression
Text copyright © 2005 by Jo & Josephine Harper
Illustrations copyright © 2005 by Ron Mazellan

First Published in 2005 by Turtle Books
All rights reserved. No part of this book may be used or reproduced in any manner whatsoever
without written permission, except in the case of brief quotations embodied in critical articles and reviews.
Turtle Books is a trademark of Turtle Books, Inc.
For information or permissions, address:
Turtle Books, 866 United Nations Plaza, Suite 525
New York, New York 10017

Cover and book design by Jessica Kirchoff
Text of this book is set in Novarese Book
Illustrations were created in oil and acrylic
First Edition
Smyth sewn, cambric reinforced binding, printed on 80#, acid-free paper
Printed and bound at Worzalla in Stevens Point, Wisconsin/U.S.A.

10 9 8 7 6 5 4 3 2 1

Library of Congress Cataloging-in-Publication Data
Harper, Jo. Finding Daddy: A Story of the Great Depression / Jo & Josephine Harper ; illustrated by Ron Mazellan.   p.   cm.
Summary: Worried he will become a burden to his family, Bonnie's out-of-work father leaves home, but Bonnie sets out with
her dog to find him and bring him home and, in the process, learns that she and her father can make money through music.
Includes glossary and photographic timeline of the Great Depression, and the words and music to
"Happy Days are Here Again."
ISBN 1-890515-31-0 (hardcover : alk. paper)
Depressions—1929—Juvenile fiction. [1. Depressions—1929—Fiction.
2. Fathers and daughters—Fiction. 3. Musicians—Fiction.]
I. Harper, Josephine, 1953-   II. Mazellan, Ron, ill. III. Title.
PZ7.H23135Fi   2005   [Fic]—dc22   2005041931

Distributed by Publishers Group West

ISBN 1-890515-31-0

FINDING DADDY:
A Story of the Great Depression

Jo & Josephine Harper

Illustrated by Ron Mazellan

Turtle Books
New York

Bonnie couldn't do it. She couldn't sing a solo at Thanksgiving Assembly. The whole school would be there. And parents. And strangers.

But Mrs. Appleby wouldn't take "no" for an answer. "Oh, Bonnie, you are such a good singer. You shouldn't stay back in the chorus. Everyone would like to hear you sing alone. Just try it here in front of the class."

Bonnie walked slowly to the front of the room. Her classmates were her friends. They all smiled. But everyone was looking at her. She could feel it. Her hands trembled. Her breath was quick, and her throat closed tight. Not a single note would come out.

Bonnie looked at the floor. She felt her face flush hot. She wanted to hide.

She shook her head and ran back to her seat.

After school, her dog—Caesar—was waiting for her at the edge of the playground. She buried her face in his warm fur. He waited for her every day. They walked home together. "You're safe with Caesar," Daddy always said.

Bonnie and Caesar played hide-and-seek with Anna and Jimmy Manning from next door. Daddy came home and joined the game. When it was Bonnie's time to be *it*, Anna and Jimmy squealed and shouted and got in free, but Bonnie saw Daddy's hat peeping out from behind the big bush at the back of the yard. She could always find Daddy.

After the game, Bonnie and Daddy walked home hand in hand, with Caesar beside them. Inside, the lights were on. Bonnie helped set the table. She put red napkins at each place. Mother had cooked hot biscuits, chicken, green beans, and apple pie.

After supper, Daddy got down his fiddle and bow. This was Bonnie's favorite time of day. Daddy played, and they sang. Sometimes Mother and Daddy sang harmony with Bonnie. Sometimes she sang alone. She wasn't shy at home.

They sang "Alexander's Ragtime Band," "The Big Rock Candy Mountain," and "In a Shanty in Old Shanty Town." The last song was "Do Re Mi." They had fun.

But things began to change at Bonnie's house. Daddy stayed home more. He was always there when Bonnie got in from school. He taught her how to play the spoons while he played the fiddle, but something felt wrong. Daddy looked worried all the time, even when he smiled.

They didn't have chicken or apple pie any more. One day they moved out of their pretty house and into a sad little house with paint peeling off the door.

It was dreary inside their new house. Bonnie felt dreary, too. *This house is a shanty* she thought.

Mother lighted an oil lamp. The light flickered softly on her face. Her eyes were very bright, and she blinked fast.

Daddy put his arm around Mother. "I'll find a job and we'll fix this old place up. I won't let you down."

Bonnie knew he was trying to sound cheerful. She wanted to help him, so she said, "Get out your fiddle, Daddy. Then it will feel like home."

"Bonnie, I sold the fiddle."

Now Bonnie blinked fast, but she couldn't keep a tear from running down her cheek.

"We can still sing together," Daddy told her.

"Sure." Bonnie forced a smile. "We don't need the fiddle. We can play the spoons." They sang "Happy Days Are Here Again," but Bonnie knew the words weren't true.

Every morning Daddy went to look for work. Some days he was gone all day, and when he came home, he gave Mother the coins he had earned. But most days, Daddy came back in a couple of hours, empty-handed.

Times were tough and there wasn't much work now. Some days Daddy sat and stared out the window. "I'm no good to you," he told Mother.

Mother began bringing other people's laundry home. She washed it on a rub board and heated irons on the stove to iron it. Daddy helped. So did Bonnie.

One day as they were hanging out clothes, a neighbor woman said loudly, "A man without a job is worse than useless. He pulls his family down. He is a burden."

Daddy's face went white. He looked as if he had been hit.

Bonnie wanted to run at that hateful woman and kick her. She wanted to hug Daddy and make him feel better. But her feet wouldn't move. She was frozen in place, frozen harder than the clean laundry freezing on the line.

Why couldn't she do something?

The next morning, Daddy kissed Mother and Bonnie good-bye. "I'll find work today," he said.

But Bonnie felt a pain in her heart. At school, she couldn't do her arithmetic, and when it was her turn to read, she whispered.

Bonnie and Caesar hurried home after school.

Daddy wasn't there.

Mother was scrubbing clothes. She nodded toward a small pan of soup on the stove. It was thin and tasteless, but Bonnie didn't care. She was worried.

Daddy didn't come home. Not all night. Not all week. Not all month.

Mother was always home, but she seemed far away. The house was dark. It was silent except for the slosh of clothes against the rub board.

No one sang.

Bonnie couldn't sleep, and the pain never left her heart. She knew it would stay with her as long as Daddy was gone.

"I can always find Daddy," she told Caesar. "I will find him this time, too!"

Bonnie and Caesar went to all the places Daddy used to go – the grocery-store – the cotton gin – the bench in the park. Daddy wasn't in any of those places. No one had seen him.

Bonnie and Caesar went to the corner where laborers gathered, hoping for work. Bonnie looked into the men's dry, set faces.

Daddy's face wasn't there.

Bonnie heard of a place outside of town where people lived in tents. She and Caesar would go there.

The wind blew in their faces as they walked. When they arrived, they saw people huddled near campfires. They went from campfire to campfire, but none of the hollow-cheeked people had seen Daddy.

"Some people found work at the port – about ten miles that way," a woman said, pointing.

Bonnie and Caesar started walking. Ten miles or fifty miles or ten thousand miles, Bonnie was going to find Daddy!

It was cold. She walked fast, and Caesar trotted. Bonnie kept her hands in her pockets.

A car pulled up beside her. She walked faster and looked straight ahead. Her heart pounded. She knew she must never get in a car with a stranger. Not even with Caesar along.

"Bonnie! Wait! Don't you know us?"

Mr. And Mrs. Manning, who used to be her neighbors, were in the car.

"Get in before you catch your death of cold," Mrs. Manning scolded gently.

Gratefully, Bonnie climbed in. Caesar jumped in after her.

"Why aren't you in school?" Mr. Manning asked.

"I have to go to the sea port. Daddy is working there," Bonnie fibbed.

Mrs. Manning raised her eyebrows. "We'll take you home to your mother."

Bonnie told another fib. "Mother's not home. Daddy will worry if I don't come."

Mr. Manning made a funny sound. It seemed to say I *don't believe you*. But he drove to the port.

"I know where to go. Thank you for the ride."

Bonnie and Caesar jumped out of the car and hurried down the street.

Bonnie's fingers were cold, and she was hungry. She knew Caesar was hungry, too.

Warm steam touched her face, and the fragrance of food drew her into a café. Bonnie peeped out the window and saw the Manning's car drive away.

The café was noisy and full of people. She needed to ask if they had seen Daddy. Bonnie knew how to do it, but she didn't think she was brave enough.

I *have to do it*. I *have to*.

Her breath was quick, and she felt her throat tighten. She put her arm around Caesar's neck, closed her eyes, and took some deep breaths.

I *can do it*. I *can, and* I *will*.

She took off her warm cap, laid it on a table, and climbed on a chair. She shook out her curls, stood up straight, and smiled.

Her hands trembled, but she started to sing. Strangers stared at her, but she kept her voice steady.

The café got quiet.

When Bonnie finished the song, people clapped. Some of them put coins in her cap. Everyone was looking.

"Have you seen my Daddy? His name is Robert Wright. He looks like me."

People shook their heads. No one had seen him.

Someone brought Bonnie a bowl of beans and a big piece of cornbread. She gave some to Caesar.

When Bonnie finished eating, she sang another song. And another. She didn't feel shy any more. More people came in and her cap was filling with coins. She liked the way people smiled and tapped their feet when she sang. And she loved the applause.

But nobody had seen Daddy.

Then Bonnie noticed that Caesar wasn't with her.

"Caesar! Caesar!" she called.

He didn't come.

Someone gestured toward the corner. "There's your dog."

Bonnie squinted and looked hard. Something moved back and forth in the darkest corner.

It was Caesar's tail wagging.

He sat beside a man who had his hat brim pulled down and a newspaper in front of his face. But the man wasn't reading. Bonnie could see his eyes peeping over the newspaper.

She jumped off the chair and ran to the back of the room.

The man put the newspaper down.
Bonnie jumped into his lap and put her arms around his neck.
It was Daddy!
She laid her head on his shoulder. She felt warm and safe.

"Daddy, you're not a burden. We need you. And I know how we can make money."

She showed Daddy the coins in her hat.

Then Bonnie and Daddy made music together. He played the spoons and sang harmony with her.

The door swung open.

Mother and the Mannings rushed in.

They all sang "Happy Days Are Here Again." This time, Bonnie knew the words were true.

Glossary of the Great Depression

Black Tuesday: October 29, 1929, the day the Wall Street stock market crashed

Civil Works Administration (CWA): A 1933-1934 federal program that hired four million Americans to build post offices and roads

Civilian Conservation Corps (CCC): A federal government program that hired two million Americans to plant trees and to create campsites in the national parks and forests

The Dust Bowl: The difficult conditions created in the south-central region of the United States when severe drought during the years 1934-1937 led to the topsoil being stripped away in dust storms

Farm Credit Administration (FCA): A federal government program to help struggling farmers refinance their farm mortgages

"Happy Days Are Here Again": 1929 song that became associated with the presidency of Franklin Delano Roosevelt (FDR)

Hoovervilles: Clusters of shanties; named after President Herbert Hoover

National Youth Administration (NYA): A part of the WPA that hired two million unemployed American students

The New Deal: The economic recovery program of President Franklin Delano Roosevelt's administration

Shanty: A makeshift shelter without electricity or running water

Soup Kitchens: Local community places where unemployed and homeless people could get some free food

Tennessee Valley Authority (TVA): A huge public works program begun in May 1933; a collection of dams and electricity-generating facilities built along the Tennessee River

Works Progress Administration (WPA): A 1935-1943 federal government program that hired unemployed American writers, actors, artists, sculptors, photographers, and researchers

Photography and Lyric Credits

PHOTOGRAPHY

Photographic Time Line of the Great Depression Era, 1929–1941

(clockwise): Bettmann/Corbis; Michael Prince/Corbis; Angelo Hornak/Corbis; Corbis; Bettmann/Corbis; AP/Wide World Photos; National Archives and Records Administration; AP/Wide World Photos; Bettmann/Corbis; Bettmann/Corbis; Historical Society of Seattle & King County/Corbis; Corbis; Bettmann/Corbis; Bettmann/Corbis; AP/Wide World Photos; Hulton-Deutsch Collection/Corbis; Bettmann/Corbis; Philip Gould/Corbis.

Authors' Note

(clockwise): Getty Images; Bettmann/Corbis; Bettmann/Corbis; John Springer Collection/Corbis; John Springer Collection/Corbis; John Springer Collection/Corbis.

Other Popular Songs of the Great Depression Period

Bettmann/Corbis

"Happy Days Are Here Again"

Photofest

LYRICS

"Happy Days Are Here Again" By: Milton Ager and Jack Yellen. © 1929 (Renewed) WB Music Corp. (ASCAP). All Rights Reserved. Used by Permission. Warner Bros. Publications U.S., Inc., Miami, FL 33014.

Authors' Note

During the period of America's Great Depression, 1929-1941, many men were so saddened by not being able to provide for their families that they abandoned them. This was also a time when some people, who had nothing but their talent to sustain them, became professional singers or actors. This story is inspired by those events and by the songs of that era.

Ella Fitzgerald (1917-1996), an improvisational 'scat' singer, won an amateur contest at Harlem's influential Apollo Theater in 1934, beginning a long, successful professional career in music.

Dickie Moore (1925-   ) and Pete the Pup charmed audiences in the popular *Our Gang* series. By the time he was ten years old, Dickie had performed in 52 films.

Judy Garland (1922-1969) made her mark in the 1939 movie, *The Wizard of Oz*, and went on to become a beloved singer.

Shirley Temple (1928-   ), delighted fans with her energetic performances.

In addition to many earlier and later movies, child actor Mickey Rooney (1920-   ) starred as the character Andy Hardy in fifteen films between 1937 and 1947.

Woody Guthrie (1912-1967), a folk singer and wandering troubadour, found his musical voice dealing with the everyday struggles of the Great Depression.

"Happy Days Are Here Again"

Lyrics by Jack Yellen

So long, sad times!
Go 'long, bad times!
We are rid of you at last.

Howdy gay times!
Cloudy gray times,
You are now a thing of the past.

'Cause happy days are here again!
The skies above are clear again.
Let us sing a song of cheer again
Happy days are here again.

Altogether shout it now!

There's no one who can doubt it now,
So let's tell the world about it now
Happy days are here again!
Your cares and troubles are gone;
There'll be no more from now on.

Happy days are here again;
The skies above are clear again;
Let us sing a song of cheer again
Happy days are here again!

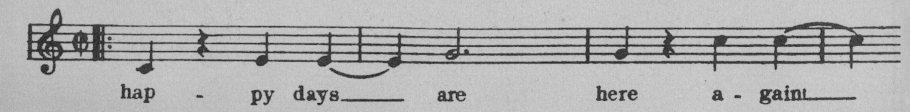

hap - py days____ are here a - gain____

Milton Ager (1893-1979) composed the music for "Happy Days Are Here Again".

Jack Yellen (1892-1991) wrote the lyrics to the 1929 song, "Happy Days Are Here Again".